Gofrette

Fat, Furry and Funny

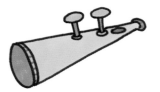

For Gofrette, Poupoune and Matisse

Editorial Director
Caroline Fortin

Graphic Design
Anne Tremblay

Page Layout
André Lambert
Lucie Mc Brearty

Copy Editor
Jane Broderick

Canadian Cataloguing in Publication Data
Brasset, Doris
Fat, Furry and Funny
(Gofrette)
For preschool children.

ISBN 2-7644-0012-8

I. Michot, Fabienne. II. Title. III. Series : Brasset, Doris. Gofrette.

PS8553.R315F37 1999   jC813'.54   C99-941199-3
PS9553.R315F37 1999
PZ7.B72Fa 1999

 QA International
329, rue de la Commune Ouest, 3e étage,
Montréal (Québec) H2Y 2E1 Canada
T 514.499.3000 F 514.499.3010
www.qa-international.com

Printed and bound in Canada

10 9 8 7 6 5 4 3 2 1 02 01 00 99

 Canada

We acknowledge the financial support of the Government
of Canada through the Book Publishing Industry
Development Program (BPIDP) for our publishing
activities.

Le Conseil des Arts | The Canada Council
du Canada | for the Arts

QAInternational gratefully acknowledges the support of :
The Canada Council for the Arts.

Gofrette
Fat, Furry and Funny
Doris Brasset and Fabienne Michot

QA INTERNATIONAL

Splish! Splash! Gofrette was taking a bath.
He was getting ready to visit his cousin
Garbanzo El Magnifico, The Circus Cat.

"Presenting the world's most amazing flying
feline! It's a bird! It's a plane! No! It's Gofrette the
Flying Furball!" He had to hurry. Blue was
coming to pick him up.

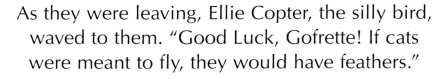

As they were leaving, Ellie Copter, the silly bird, waved to them. "Good Luck, Gofrette! If cats were meant to fly, they would have feathers."

A few hours and many miles later, the circus tent appeared before them like a rainbow. It stood tall and colourful like a promise in the sky, rising above their great expectations.

Gofrette and Blue now had to find Garbanzo's caravan. Greta the Gorgeous Gorilla pointed them in the right direction. Blue was impressed by her muscles. Gofrette liked her outfit.

"Ah...Magnifico! You have arrived just in time for lunch. Come in, quickly!" exclaimed a delighted Garbanzo.

Garbanzo, also known as Garbo, served them each a big bowl of spaghetti. Blue and Gofrette slurped up the scrumptious sauce.

"I hope you have practiced your magic tricks and trapezing,
because tomorrow is THE BIG DAY!" said Garbanzo.

Life is a
balancing
act.

Lunch was over and trouble was about
to begin. Garbanzo grabbed Gofrette and Blue,
swung them onto his shoulders and brought
them to the tent.

Inside, the Five Fabulous Fusilli Brothers were
rehearsing their balancing act. Gofrette was
impressed. "It's a good thing there's no wind
in here," said Blue.

Circus philosophy
1. Not all clowns wear costumes.
2. The real clowns aren't in the circus.
3. Everybody's got a cousin in the circus.

It was now Blue and Gofrette's turn to show
Garbanzo what they had practiced at home.
Blue was perfect, swinging through the air
like a bluebird.

Gofrette took a deep breath and swung forward.
The world was a fine place to live,
even upside down.

With practice over, Gofrette and Blue
could now sit and watch the other animals;
one bird was chirping, two fish were kissing,
three lions were singing, four purple seals...

That night, the two fidgety friends held paws
and wished each other luck for the next day
– THE BIG DAY. Garbanzo was fast asleep,
snoring like a pig with a cold.

THE BIG DAY WAS HERE. Gorgeous Greta greeted everyone.
"WELCOME! WELCOME, ALL YOU FUZZY FRIENDS! TODAY YOU WILL

SEE A SPECTACLE BEYOND BELIEF! STEP RIGHT UP, STEP RIGHT IN..."
They filled the tent until it was like a mouth full of bubblegum ready to burst.

Inside, Garbanzo was making the presentations.
"Welcome! Today you will see the most amazing
and dangerous tricks ever performed. Let's start
the show with our very own...Edith the Penguin,
Purple the Dog and the Dandy Lions performing,
for your pleasure, death-defying balancing acts!"

Then came Blue. "I will now saw this fat feline in two. Drum roll, please!" **DRRRR...DRRRR...** It was easy to see this sawing-in-half trick was making Gofrette very nervous.

"TA-DAH!" The trick worked and the crowd cheered! Of course, Blue knew the secret magic formula that could put Gofrette back together again. "Pst...pss...pss...glue...pss...pst..."

Humpty Dumpty had it easy.

The most dangerous part of the show was about to begin.
It was a swoop-and-scoop-me-through-the-air-swing-your-partner-

round-and-round-fling-your-partner-upside-down trapeze act.
Greta, Garbo, Gofrette and Blue swung through the air.

Up was down and down was up...

Gorgeous Greta grasped Blue! Gofrette
grabbed Garbanzo...
by the mustache! **OUCH!!!**

The band down below burst into a loud
OOMPAH OOMPAH OOMPAPAH!

They had done it!

Gofrette jumped on the unicycle and onto the high wire.
Halfway across, Greta shouted, **"GOFRETTE! BE CAREFUL! THERE'S A**

FLY ON THE WIRE!" With all the loud music and clapping, Gofrette heard,
"GOFRETTE! YOU'RE WONDERFUL! YOU CAN FLY EVEN HIGHER!"

Greta was right. Gofrette hit the fly, the fly flew
away, the pins fell...all eyes were on him.

Gofrette came tumbling down, knocking one
of the Five Fabulous Fusilli Brothers off his horse.
The crowd gasped and then exploded with
laughter.! This was the greatest flying cat trick
they had ever seen!

Late into the night the Fabulous Flying
Furry Friends danced and sang, celebrating
Gofrette's new-found talent. Gofrette's amazing
CAT-astrophe was never to be forgotten.